A NEIGHBORHOOD WALK, A MUSICAL JOURNEY

Pilar Winter Hill

illustrated by Olivia Duchess

Albert Whitman & Company
Chicago, Illinois

Mom, Dad, Sis, and Brother Bear...You are the best
...mily a girl dreamer could ever have!—PWH

...o Mum, who always made sure there was music in
...he house. And to my best pal, Funbi.—OD

Library of Congress Cataloging-in-Publication data
is on file with the publisher.
Text copyright © 2021 by Pilar Winter Hill
Illustrations copyright © 2021 by Albert Whitman & Company
Illustrations by Olivia Duchess
First published in the United States of America in 2021
by Albert Whitman & Company
ISBN 978-0-8075-3670-4 (hardcover)
ISBN 978-0-8075-3668-1 (ebook)

Printed in China
10 9 8 7 6 5 4 3 2 1 WKT 24 23 22 21 20

Design by Valerie Hernández

For more information about Albert Whitman & Company,
visit our website at www.albertwhitman.com.

Honk-honk! Tweet-tweet! Patter-patter! Penelope's eyes open
to the sound of the city.

Down the steps she bounces, toward the smell of Saturday breakfast.

Penelope chomps through pancakes, and Mom grabs a tote bag.
It's Farmers Market Day!

Penelope can picture the market, full of peaches and strawberries, and maybe ice cream too.

Just off the stoop, there's noise in the air.

A golden instrument reflects the sun into their eyes. A man sways to the rhythm of his saxophone with a *toot-a-toot-swoosh!*

They stay awhile, watching his cheeks fill with air.
Penelope is wrapped up in brassy melodies and—*screech*!
A bus is rushing by.

They continue with a wave. He winks as they pass.
One block closer to a fresh, sweet feast.

A few streets later, Mom stops. Her foot taps.

Boom-bam-boom-boom. A drum cuts through the noisy rumblings of the subway station.

The sound is big, fast, and exciting; Penelope starts to move!

The drummer's hands are flying, *tap-tapping*, *tap-tapping* on
the drum. Penelope claps and stomps to the beat, but *whoosh!*
The train is here. She hops on and checks the shopping list.

They stop for a moment at the florist. The flowers are in full bloom. Vibrations catch Penelope's ear: *flutter-flutter-whiz.*

A flautist flings fast notes that sound like the flapping of butterfly wings. Penelope is buzzing to the rhythm.

Ring! Ring! A biker flashes past, and they're already skipping down the sidewalk.

They pass through the park under fluttering trees.
Penelope peeks through a crowd to see a little boy
prancing along to the twang of an acoustic guitar.

The musician strums with passion as the boy
twirls, but Mom can't see him dancing through all
the people. They don't stop!

Twang-thump-twang. His sweet music follows Penelope back to the street.

Outside the bakery, Mom runs into a neighbor. Penelope slumps as they talk, until a cellist's *pluck-pluck-pluck* floats down from a window above. His bow glides on the strings, and the deep sound pulls her into a dream.

Mom says goodbye to her friend. Penelope is sad to hear those strong notes fade away.

Finally, the market! They walk along, filling the tote. Penelope wonders what ice-cream flavor to pick, when suddenly, there's a sound.

She looks up and down and hangs on to the distant note.

It starts slow and grows bolder. It picks up tempo as if taking flight. Penelope searches for the music through wandering shoppers.

Price
List

Sellers offer samples. Children shout. A fountain splashes nearby.
But still, the sound rings out.

A violinist stands around the bend. She's electrifying her instrument with each fiery note. *Zing-whiz-hum-ding!*

A spark inside Penelope ignites as she stands in the flurry of sound. *Ding-hum-zing-zing!* Time slows, and the music freezes her all the way down to her toes.

All the other sounds fade away.

Penelope imagines holding the violin and learning to play those whirring notes. This magical instrument is calling her to listen.

"I can feel those notes," she thinks.
"I'm going to make that music too."

Author's Note

I was drawn to the violin as a very young child; as if by magic, it just called to me. Something wonderful stirred inside me from the moment I first heard the beautiful sound of someone playing. I knew I was meant to play too. I have now been playing the violin for eight years. The connection between my instrument and me has always been strong and constant. It's kind of like breathing. I practice for many hours every day and spend lots of time working on material in preparation for exciting performances all around the world. I wrote this story to not only celebrate the special moment when I first discovered my love of music, but also to show the excitement that music all around us provides. The idea of being able to share my love of music with young people around the globe truly makes me happy; music feels personal and shared at the same time. It is universal.